To Eddie, the Baby Woolly of our bunch! xx —K.M^CK.
To my woollie consultants Harry, Ellie and Meggie —J.S.

OXFORD
UNIVERSITY PRESS

Great Clarendon Street, Oxford OX2 6DP

Oxford University Press is a department of the University of Oxford.
It furthers the University's objective of excellence in research, scholarship,
and education by publishing worldwide.

Oxford is a registered trade mark of Oxford University Press in the UK and in
certain other countries

Text © Oxford University Press 2018
Illustrations © Jon Stuart 2018

The moral rights of the author/illustrator have been asserted Database right
Oxford University Press (maker)

First published in 2018

British Library Cataloguing in Publication Data
Data available

ISBN: 978-0-19-276668-7 (paperback)

10 9 8 7 6 5 4 3 2 1

Printed in China

Paper used in the production of this book is a natural, recyclableproduct made
from wood grown in sustainable forests.The manufacturing process conforms to
the environmental regulations of the country of origin.

THE WOOLLIES

Join the Parade!

OXFORD
UNIVERSITY PRESS

Kelly McKain
Jon Stuart

The Woollies were snoozing by their house.

Something tickled Baby Woolly . . .
and woke him up!

'Where did these little flags come from, Zip?' puffed Baby Woolly, jumping up high.
'They are from the parade yesterday,' said Zip.

Baby Woolly grinned. 'We could have our own **Woolly** Parade!' 'Good idea,' said Zip. 'Imagi-knit!'

Boom, boom, boom went the big bass drum.
Dee de lee de lee went the banjo.

Chooka chooka chooka went the maracas.
Baby Woolly led the parade!

Jingle! Jingle!

When the Woollies stopped for a rest,
Baby Woolly leapt on to the drum.
'Can I have a go now?' he asked.
'Please be careful!' Zip gasped.

But it was too late! Baby Woolly rolled away down the slope. Faster and faster and faster! 'Quick, imagi-knit!' cried his friends.

'We're coming!' cried Bling, Puzzle, and Zip.
But they couldn't see Baby Woolly anywhere!

Luckily, Baby Woolly was OK.
'My Woolly friends will catch up soon!'
he said. 'I'm going to surprise them!
Imagi-knit!'

'Now I'm a big parade dragon!' Baby Woolly shouted.
'Wait till I show Puzzle and Bling and Zip!'

But - oh, no! The dragon was too heavy! Baby Woolly got stuck!

Suddenly the other Woollies saw lots of bright flames!

'Oh no – a fire!' gasped Puzzle.
'Let's go and put it out!' cried Bling.
'Imagi-knit!'

Nee-naw, nee-naw, nee-naw!
'Fast as you can, Zip!'

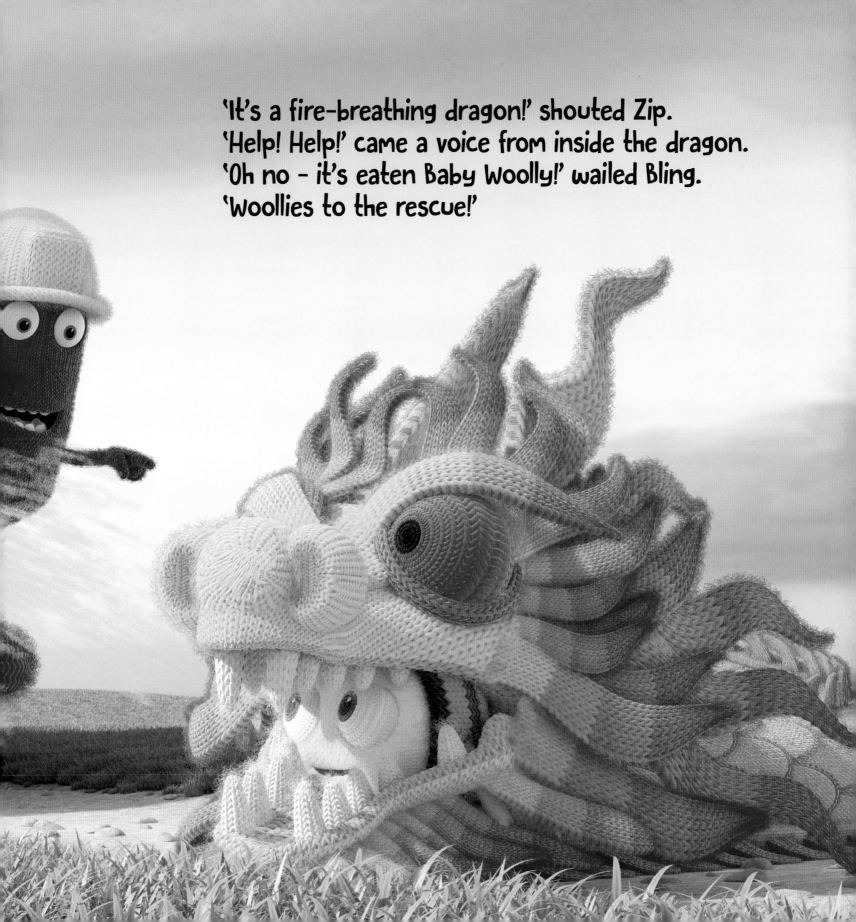

'It's a fire-breathing dragon!' shouted Zip.
'Help! Help!' came a voice from inside the dragon.
'Oh no - it's eaten Baby Woolly!' wailed Bling.
'Woollies to the rescue!'

'So it wasn't a real dragon after all!' cried Zip.
Baby Woolly laughed. 'No, it wasn't! And now
I am a very soggy Woolly!'

'Whoops!' giggled Bling. 'Don't worry, the sun will soon dry you out!'

Now everyone was a dragon!
The Woollies sang all the way home.

'I'm tired!' yawned Baby Woolly.
'Nap time for baby bees . . . '

A note for grown-ups

Oxford Owl is a FREE and easy-to-use website packed with support and advice about everything to do with reading.

Informative videos

Hints, tips and fun activities

Top tips from top writers for reading with your child

Help with choosing picture books

For this expert advice and much, much more about how children learn to read and how to keep them reading ...

LO,OK
for Oxford Owl
www.oxfordowl.co.uk